Vo started to gather up the things on the table. The portable computer and light-pen went into his backpack, along with an old-fashioned paper notebook barely bigger than his hand and honest-to-Creator ink pen.

"You're leaving already?" Phoebe asked, maybe a little hurt.

Vo stood up and grabbed his jacket. Civilian attire was still alien, but Quinta had mild winters, so he didn't need anything heavy.

"Almost time for class," he said.

It was a good way to extract himself from a confusing situation.

Phoebe grabbed her things and stood as well.

"I'll walk with you to class," she announced, a queen bestowing a favor on her favorite champion.

What the hell have I done to warrant this sort of attention?

SIREN

AN ALEXANDRIA STATION STORY

BLAZE WARD

ALSO BY BLAZE WARD

The Jessica Keller Chronicles
Auberon
Queen of the Pirates
Last of the Immortals

Javier Aritza Stories
The Science Officer
The Mind Field
The Gilded Cage

Additional Alexandria Station Stories
The Story Road
Greater Than The Gods Intended
The Librarian

Other Science Fiction Stories
Mymirdons
Moonshot
Earthquake Gun
Moscow Gold

The Collective Universe
Imposters
The Shipwrecked Mermaid

Collections
Beyond the Mirror: Volume 1 Fantastic Worlds
Beyond the Mirror: Volume 2 Fantastic Worlds
Beyond the Mirror: Volume 3 Alternate Worlds

SIREN

AN ALEXANDRIA STATION STORY

BLAZE WARD

Knotted Road Press
www.KnottedRoadPress.com

I

Date of the Republic October 4, 394 Quinta City, Quinta

The girl's voice knocked Vo out of his reverie and brought him back to the present.

"Hey, Vo," she called as she walked up to his table in the Student Union. "Finn tells me you used to be in the navy?"

He looked up from the woman on the screen of his portable computer and considered the girl standing across from him. The two looked nothing alike, this one a busty, beautiful brunette and the one on the screen a skinny blond that some might call homely. The only thing they had in common was height.

This one was about to plop down into one of the other chairs at his table, so her head was down. He was used to analyzing someone for risk and competence at a glance, the downside of eight years active duty as a fleet security marine. Even pretty girls in a student union hall.

What was her name? Fevre? F-something? Phoebe. That was it.

Phoebe was tall for a girl and busty in a very distracting way. He wasn't sure she was wearing anything under that green sweater as she took off her coat and hung it from the chair across from him. The way her chest moved suggested not, but he couldn't tell for certain and didn't want to stare.

Vo checked the time on his personal comm as Phoebe sat, but the clock in his head was still accurate enough. He'd supposedly been reviewing his accounting homework and reading ahead, but he still had at least ten minutes before he needed to pack up and go to class.

"Still am," he said, unable to figure out why the prettiest girl in class suddenly wanted to chat him up.

It wasn't like he was particularly good looking. His previous bosses had frequently picked him for assignments because he was nearly two meters tall, incredibly strong, and looked like a street hoodlum. That could generally be considered an asset in his line of work.

"Are what?" she asked, perplexed as she sat down and dropped a heavy backpack of books and stuff beside her.

"I'm still on active duty," he replied.

That didn't help. She got an even more confused look on her face. She had really pretty green eyes.

"But you're a student," she said, her voice starting to edge into a whine. "You're in my business accounting class."

"I'm on detached duty for this semester," he replied. "Reward from my boss, and using up all my leave, and a few other things."

"So what ship are you on?" she inquired with a grin, leaning onto the table in a way that did distracting things under the sweater.

Vo caught his breath and brought his eyes back up to hers.

"None, right now," he replied heavily. "The old one got decommissioned. The new one's not done being built yet. Boss owed me a favor. Plus I'm kinda on medical rehab. It all added up to enough time to take some classes."

"Medical rehab?"

The confusion was back.

"I got shot up pretty bad, last time out," he said in a tone that suggested she not ask further questions. "The ship was *Auberon*."

Her eyes lit up. It was a good way to distract people.

"Jessica Keller?" she probed sharply.

Vo nodded. Everyone knew *RAN Auberon* and her very famous Command Centurion. He could bask a little in that glory. He had actually been on *Alexandria Station* until about twenty minutes before the Red Admiral blew it up at *Ballard* four months ago.

Still, he had figured that someplace as remote as *Quinta*, and a college like the Quinta Colonial Institute, would have been far enough away from the main byways of the Republic. There was almost no Fleet presence here, and no Marines groundside. He could pretend to be a civilian for five months.

Or could have. He probably shouldn't have told Finn anything, but the kid had a good heart and had been genuinely interested in the older guy in class.

Older? Gods, this girl across from me is probably younger than my youngest sister, Sonja.

"I bet you could tell me some awesome stories about her," Phoebe said, her eyes all aglitter.

"Maybe later," Vo shrugged. "Supposed to go get lunch with Finn after class and talk mid-terms. Then I need to write a history paper tonight."

Vo started to gather up the things on the table. The portable computer and light-pen went into his backpack, along with an old-fashioned paper notebook barely bigger than his hand and honest-to-Creator ink pen.

"You're leaving already?" she asked, maybe a little hurt.

Vo stood up and grabbed his jacket. Civilian attire was still alien, but Quinta had mild winters, so he didn't need anything heavy.

"Almost time for class," he said.

It was a good way to extract himself from a confusing situation.

Phoebe grabbed her things and stood as well.

"I'll walk with you to class," she announced, a queen bestowing a favor on her favorite champion.

What the hell have I done to warrant this sort of attention?

Vo had hoped that picking a table on the restaurant's patio would dissuade Phoebe from staying long at lunch. It hadn't worked, but at least she had stayed bundled up in her heavy jacket and he wasn't being distracted by her chest.

As much.

Less than Finn, anyway.

They had the space mostly to themselves, another twenty minutes or so before the serious lunch rush came. Vo had ended up facing the empty chair, with Finn on his right and Phoebe on his left.

Hot chocolate and coffee had always mixed well as a cheap way to get warm calories in the field. Today felt close enough to a planetary drop to qualify. Maybe worse. Planetary assaults didn't normally leave him so nervous.

Pretty women did that to him.

The woman, no, let's face it, girl, was honestly batting her eyes at him. All he could think of was *fleet groupie*, but even that was a stretch. She wasn't some poor farm girl on a dead-end planet looking for any way out.

He had known a few of those along the way.

Vo knew that her mother was the mayor of her home town, and her father was a business exec of some sort, but that was about as much as he had been able to pick up. This girl probably had the whole planet to pick from, and potentially the whole Republic if she really wanted.

She didn't need him to escape. And this planet was good enough for his needs.

Quinta Colonial Institute wasn't the top college on the planet, but it was in the top five for business schools. And it accepted transfer credits from the *RAN*, the *Republic of Aquitaine Navy*. One semester ground-side and he would have a Class I degree.

Then he could be an officer. And then *she* might notice him. Or rather, she might smile at him with warmth instead of just noticing him and going on with her day.

"What about you, Vo?" Finn asked.

Vo went blank. He had been lost in the recesses of his head, thinking about pretty girls back home who were way out of his league, kinda like the one beside him.

"Huh?" he replied intelligently.

"What are you going to do after you graduate, man?" Finn asked with an exasperated sigh.

Vo hadn't made many friends here. He was only going to be local for the one semester, and then off-planet again. Hadn't seemed worth the effort.

"Back to Fleet," he replied. "Hopefully become an officer. Retire in another twenty or twenty-five years and go into business."

"Do you know what ship you'll be on?" Phoebe asked sweetly. She leaned forward again and did something with crossed arms that made her chest stand out. Her eyes got a bright green glitter as well.

How did pretty girls do that? Very distracting. Dangerously so. Why me?

Vo took a sip of hot liquid to stop the first words from coming out his mouth. *Auberon*'s Dragoon, *Navin the Black*, had pounded that lesson into his head.

Never say the first words.

"Supposedly, they'll be commissioning a new *Auberon* for Keller," he said. "Don't know, this far from *Ladeux*."

"So you're not here for long?" she asked wistfully.

Wistfully? What the hell?

"No, ma'am," Vo replied, dropping back into a lifetime of training. "Here to do a job and then on to the next. What about you?"

He watched her lean back and get a far-away look in her eyes. She suddenly looked much younger. Almost fragile.

"Two options," she said quietly. "Stay here and be the biggest fish in a small pond. Or try my luck in the big, bad galaxy."

Vo could agree with that. Of course, his primary options at her age most likely had him dead or in prison by now. But these two bright, innocent, middle-class kids didn't need to know what growing up in the slums of Anameleck Prime was like. A neighborhood like Z'Shani was way more dangerous than they could imagine, much less survive for long.

"Finn?" Vo asked, steering the conversation back to his only real friend on the planet.

"Business, man," he said with a smile that lit up his face. Finn had a golden-brown tinge to his skin and black hair that he had explained as *Thai*. Whatever that meant. Apparently, it was a Homeworld thing.

Vo was a mutt, he didn't come from a culture, so much as a place. And not a particularly nice place.

"I'm the first kid in my family to go to college," Finn continued, animation growing in his whole body. "Gonna get a job with a desk instead of a shovel for a few years, then go into business for myself."

Vo started to say something else, but Finn suddenly looked at his comm.

"Crap, I gotta go," he said, hastily pulling a few bills from a pocket and handing them to Vo. "Supposed to work extra hours this afternoon. See you Wednesday?"

"Will do," Vo replied to Finn's back.

And suddenly, he was alone with the girl. At least as alone as you could be in a restaurant with only a handful of other early birds for lunch and a waitress running around. Close enough.

He kind of stared at her for a second. Saying something like *So now what?* was too much like an open invitation.

Dangerously thin ice.

He would be here on this planet for another two months, and then gone forever. And this certainly wasn't the girl whose picture was on his personal computer screen.

He decided to retreat.

Vo pulled out his wallet and added a couple more bills on top of Finn's pile, watching Phoebe like a rabbit suddenly spotting a hawk overhead.

Quickly, he slid his chair back and stood up, grabbing his bag and his jacket.

"I need to write a history paper this afternoon," he announced carefully, preemptively, defensively.

Phoebe moved faster than he could escape.

She rose as well. He could just sit all day and watch her move. She had studied ballet or something from a young age. She had that same smooth physicality as Navin the Black, without being an ogre marine commander.

Command Centurion Keller, back on *Auberon*, moved in a whole different manner, but she was a master of *Valse d'Glaive*, the waltz of swords, and it showed. Night and day.

Before he could take a step, Phoebe laid a hand on his forearm. Nothing more than that, but nothing less than that, either.

"I've always wanted to learn archery, Vo," she said, out of the blue. "Could you teach me?"

She withdrew her hand, but the feeling lingered on his skin, even through the jacket.

"Archery?" Vo countered, utterly confused. "How did you know…?"

"Finn told me," she replied quickly. "He was bragging you up the other day and mentioned it."

"Oh," Vo said, thinking furiously. "I wouldn't even know where to find gear around here."

"Leave that to me," she said with sudden warmth. "This weekend?"

"Sure," Vo nodded, a little lost, but closer to safe ground. He hoped.

She relaxed from tension that hadn't been evident until it was gone.

"Thank you, Vo," she smiled, pulling her own money out and adding it to the pile. "See you Wednesday?"

"Yes, ma'am."

And then she was gone. At least her coat was short enough that he could enjoy her bottom as she walked away. It was a nice bottom.

Still, what the hell was it about him that excited a woman like that?

Vo looked at the time. Several hours gone. Late enough to consider bed. The paper was almost done, but for the conclusions and cleanup. And it wasn't due until the end of the semester, another seven weeks or so. On that distant weekend, he would be packing to return to his real life, while everyone else was in a panicked mode trying to write something halfway passable.

He had switched to decaf tea when he started working on the paper. He looked up now at his tiny apartment, two blocks from campus, and marveled. Students would probably bitch at being asked to live, to survive, in just thirty square meters. On the ship, he would have shared it with three other Yeomen. Or five First-Rate Spacers.

Perceptions.

Something kept niggling at the back of his mind.

Archery.

He had never mentioned archery to Finn.

After *Ballard*, he was supposed to take six months off from all physical training while all his muscles healed. No Kendo, no archery, no close combat training. Nothing beyond merely practicing his forms every day to maintain flexibility and muscle memory.

Hell, he wasn't even supposed to engage in sex until the doctors cleared him. Let all the core muscles recover, without strain, or he'd be risking a medical discharge in another three to five years.

The shot from the saboteur on *Alexandria Station* had drilled him dead center, right in his trauma plate.

Idiot. That was why Marines wore the damned things.

It had shattered, like it was supposed to, absorbing fire that would have splattered him otherwise. But in doing do, all the muscles in his stomach and chest had sustained major damage.

Vo had too much to do to start over without a full pension and a lot of lead time planned in. It was how he worked.

So he was pretty sure he hadn't mentioned archery to Finn. Or Phoebe. Or anyone else on this planet. How had she known about it?

II

Date of the Republic October 9, 394 Quinta City, Quinta

Vo had seriously considered showing up on the medical report this morning. Calling in sick. Whatever civilians called it. Had wrestled with his conscience with it since he woke up.

Still, he had promised Phoebe he'd do this. Kinda. Agreed with her on Monday. And Wednesday. And Friday. Friday, she'd made it a point to sit next to him at the lecture, putting Finn on her other side.

So here he was. He hadn't even known about the Quinta Athletic Club, or whatever it was, until she gave him directions and made sure he knew he was on the guest list.

Guest List.

It was an imposing door. The kind that screamed *Money* to a kid from the slums. Rich folk. Not Fifty Families rich, but the local aristocracy on this planet.

At least his civilian clothes looked reasonable. It felt like the kind of place where he should take his hat off to enter, had he been wearing one. Instead, he had gray dungarees, a royal blue undershirt, and a green Henley shirt. The only thing Fleet about him was his boots, comfy and waterproof.

Inside, he found a lobby done in marble tile and old, stained wood. More money.

A very young girl, maybe sixteen, sat behind a counter and smiled politely up at him.

"May I help you, sir?" she asked.

"Vo Arlo," he replied, fighting not to snap to attention. "I'm on the guest list?"

She looked down for a moment, smiled up at him, and lifted a receiver.

"Miss Akkersdijk," she said into it. "Your guest is here. Yes. Thank you."

She put the comm down and smiled.

"She'll be right up."

"Thank you."

Vo moved to one side and asked himself again what he was doing in a place like this. Maybe he needed to be more of a coward, occasionally.

Phoebe emerged from an inner door, almost hidden behind a pillar across the way, before he could think of anything more intelligent. She was in tight slacks and the kind of sleeveless blouse competition shooters frequently wore, all in a soft brown the color of winter trees, with a long-sleeved green shirt underneath. Her luxurious brown hair was pulled back into a complicated braid thingee that looked like it probably required a team of professionals to accomplish.

"Vo," she smiled as she approached. She was tall for a girl. He was still a head and a half taller. She settled for wrapping her arms around his chest and pressing her breasts flat against his stomach in a hug. "I'm so glad you could make it."

He half-hugged her back, trying not to be overwhelmed by her scent. It was pine and flowers and spring and lovely.

She leaned back enough to make eye contact.

"Ready?"

Not the least bit, young lady.

But he couldn't say that out loud. Tough guy, don't you know.

"Sure."

"This way," she said, mostly letting go but grabbing his hand, and leading him back through the door.

The weather was still mild at this latitude, so she took him quickly through the building and out a side door to a long, skinny, dedicated outdoor archery range. Hunting wasn't big on this planet, apparently, so they had the entire place to themselves.

Lovely.

Vo settled for examining the equipment she had brought.

He hadn't been sure what to expect. Archery could mean so many things to people, from traditional English Yew all the way to up exotic, tiny compound bows that looked like slingshots turned on their sides.

Today, she had what his instructors had called a Japanese Greatbow, a daikyū. It was an asymmetric style, almost a double recurve, shaped vaguely like the letter W, intended to stick up several feet over your head when you fired it, unlike a shorter, more classical version that was just bowed in the middle. And it was expensive, a multi-layer bamboo laminate done in the ancient style. At least it was already strung, so he didn't have to find a tool to bow it properly.

Vo picked up a bracer sized for a woman with small-around arms. It looked like a toy in his hands, but it would protect her entire forearm when she fired.

He felt like an ogre next to her. More like one than before.

She was suddenly close enough to smell again, though not quite rubbing up against his side, as long as he didn't move suddenly.

Arlo, you are certified to teach small arms, long arms, explosives, and close combat. You've taught female marines all of these things. Pull yourself together.

He couldn't ever remember a shave-tail marine broadcasting an almost-palpable desire like this. Not for him. One of the pretty boys, sure. Never the thug.

He took a step sideways and turned, holding the bracer out like a tower shield to protect himself from the barbarian hordes.

"Put this on first," he said firmly.

Drill instructor he could do.

She nearly defeated him by merely holding out her left arm.

"How?"

Shut up and soldier, marine.

Vo turned her arm over carefully and strapped the pseudo-leather in place. Real leather would be stiffer. This was still new-in-box smelling. The finger-straps for her shooting hand were too, but they were obvious in function when he handed them to her.

At least the blouse she was wearing worked to press her chest flat enough to keep her breasts out of the way when she shot. And her hair was back. He wouldn't have to touch her much.

Have to.

Vo took a breath and pulled several arrows from a bucket at his feet. Brand new black shafts, with red and orange fletching. Laser straight, and not a single scratch on them. He rarely got new ones on the ship, except when he shot the old ones to pieces and then bribed the machine shop to melt them down and cast him new ones.

Might as well start on the ten meter target.

It looked like an elk. At least what the books said an elk looked like. City-boy had never seen one in the wild. The only things he had ever hunted had been on two legs.

Vo pulled the Greatbow from the vertical holder and reached out a hand to pull Phoebe to the firing line.

She had back muscles under that blouse. The kind that weren't obvious unless you touched them, or saw them. For a moment, he imagined what she looked like without the blouse on, using only his fingers in the dark to see her.

He cleared his throat and concentrated on her feet.

"Turn your hips to the right seventy degrees," he ordered, falling into his role of marine instructor. "Shift your feet with them, shoulder width apart."

She came close. He used his own feet to tap hers into the placement he wanted.

It was almost like slow-dancing, her back pressed up against his stomach. Vo took a deep breath and handed her the bow as he stepped back.

"Grab an arrow and rest it on that little shelf," he continued, pointing from his safe observation post.

Watching her bend over to retrieve an arrow didn't help his concentration. At least, not to the task at hand.

"The arrow is notched at the rear," he said. "Place that on the string, just above the little metal ring and hook it on."

Hopefully, someone had done at least a preliminary job of sighting the bow in. If not, he could probably find the tools to do it himself.

At last, she was ready.

Vo pantomimed the draw and the shot.

"Hold your right arm back, pointed at the target," he explained. "Keep your left hand loose. You'll push forward with it, so don't grip the bow, except to hold it in place."

She came close. He had to step in and align her stance, a finger here, a palm there.

It was a good thing it was cool out. He was starting to sweat.

"Hold the string with your first two fingers like this," he showed her. "Take a breath, pull back to your cheek, hold for a single count, and let go. Keep your eyes on the red spot."

She flexed her shoulders. It went all the way down to her thighs.

Muscles. Nice muscles. Gymnast, perhaps. Maybe swimmer. Certainly not a couch potato.

At ten meters, she didn't miss the red dot by much. Close enough to kill a squirrel that was stupid enough to sit still for it. Most of them were.

"Now what?" she asked, glancing back over her shoulder.

"Again," he said.

Parade rest felt safe. Navin the Black did that when he was observing technique. Results came from practice.

She bent down for another arrow. Nocked it. Breathed. Fired.

"Again," he commanded.

Watching her move might be an interesting new hobby, all by itself.

"All of them?" she asked nervously.

"You won't have any habits yet, marine," he growled. "We'll fix the bad ones as they come up."

"Oh."

She fired. He watched. Whatever else she was up to, at least she was willing to work.

Most of the afternoon had fled. Vo found himself in the lounge, or restaurant, or whatever they called it in a joint like this. He had never been to an Athletic Club before. It felt close enough to country clubs he had read about.

They had eaten a fantastic early dinner, all good cuts of meat and fresh veggies.

Vo kept both hands wrapped tightly around a mug of hot tea as the waiter cleared the table. He wasn't that cold, but Phoebe had a look like she might want to hold his hand if he put it down.

He was still pretty sure that would be a dumb idea on his part.

Still, the girl had worked her butt off, today. Twenty-four arrows in the bucket. Fire them all. Walk over, pull them out manually, however deep they were driven into the target. Walk back. Fire them again. Repeat ten times.

Even he would be feeling it in the shoulders and kidneys now. Of course, she was using a bow strung to around fifteen kilograms, when his normal draw weight was thirty-six.

But she hadn't complained once.

What the hell did she want from him that she would suffer that level of work cheerfully and silently? Most of his marines would have been bitching halfway through.

"So now what?" she asked quietly as she put down her glass of iced lemonade.

Indeed, young lady. Now what?

Vo shrugged as nonchalantly as he could. The thin ice was back.

"My recommendation would be a massage," he said. "Followed by a good hot soak to flush the muscles. Maybe a glass of wine after that. Sleep for twelve hours."

"Do you do massage?" she asked with a less-than-innocent smile. And a mischievous glitter in those intelligent, green eyes.

Arlo, when are you going to learn to keep your mouth shut around pretty girls?

"It's only fair," she continued slyly, with just that perfect tilt to the head. "You did this to me. You should have to fix it."

Not the logic he would have traced, but she did have a point. And maybe, just maybe, a little wine would loosen her up to the point she'd give him some clues as to why the sudden interest in the big, brute marine.

And seriously, how often did a pretty girl come on to a guy like him?

Vo nodded, kinda. It would certainly be a better evening than going back to his efficiency apartment and reading biographies of famous Imperial admirals, which had been the original plan.

"I suppose," he began.

"Great," she said, immediately standing up with a smile. "Let's go."

"Now?"

"Yes, silly," she glared down at him seriously. "If we wait too long, I won't be able to move."

And I might just change my mind on the overall stupidity of the topic.

Arlo understood how the woodchuck in the cartoon felt, right at that moment when the snow gave way and turned everything into an avalanche under her feet. The animators always stretched it out enough to give her a moment to break the fourth wall and say something to the kids watching.

He didn't have any pithy observations.

If the Athletic Club had been money, her flat was class. Vo could only imagine how much it would have cost just to decorate the place. A whole bunch of his paychecks.

He didn't have a ground transport, so he had been relying on a good bus schedule and a lot of walking to get around. Phoebe had a bright red sportster that seemed to be two seats, four wheels, and a big engine.

At least she drove it like she knew what she was doing.

Her apartment was in a tower in the expensive part of town, with secured parking underneath and doors to code through in three places just to get her floor. She wasn't in the penthouse, but Vo felt like he could see forever out the big picture window in the living room.

Around him, two big chairs and a side table to the right and a sofa on the left, framing a fireplace that looked real. At least the wood piled to one side was. Expensive pictures on the walls, bric-a-brac on every flat surface, and carpet that felt deep enough to hide large predators.

Other large predators.

He turned around as she came back from the bedroom.

She had changed out of her expensive shooting outfit, and was wearing a fuzzy, gray robe.

He really hoped she was wearing something under it.

"Ready?" she asked with a bright smile.

Vo's boots were already by the door, and his jacket hung up in a closet. He was probably pretty much trapped at this point.

"Sure," he agreed, talking himself into this.

It still felt like a bad idea. He kept waiting for her parents or someone to come home and catch them, like that time he and Janny had been necking on the couch.

Nobody did.

She turned and headed back into the bedroom. He followed, understanding how the bull felt on the way to the sacrificial altar.

She was standing beside a giant bed that was covered by a heavy comforter, with a small stuffed tiger tucked in among the throw pillows. At least everything was blues.

He had been unconsciously steeling himself for lots of pink.

"How did you want me?" she asked with an innocence in her voice that never made it to her eyes.

Shut up and soldier, marine.

Vo took a deep breath and considered the logistics of the room.

"Face down on the bed," he replied. "Without the robe."

"Okay," she smiled.

It felt like slow motion, but it wasn't. He just preferred to remember it at that speed.

Phoebe opened the robe and let it drop at her feet. At least she was wearing a pair of loose, green shorts.

Nothing else. Just the shorts.

And her chest was every bit as impressive as he had imagined.

She turned and stretched out on the bed, her arms up and her wrists crossed under her forehead.

It took Vo a couple of seconds for the static to clear from his brain.

Seriously, what the hell was wrong with him?

He moved to the side of the bed and studied her. Her breasts were squished flat against the comforter in ways that were probably more distracting than they should have been. And there were no tan lines visible.

The only girls he had ever seen without tan lines were professionals. Dancers, or entertainers, or whatever the hell they wanted to call themselves.

He made a note not to mention that on this planet.

"Lotion is on the night table," she murmured in his general direction.

Vo walked around to that side and picked it up.

It smelled safe enough. Coconut and vanilla. It probably would come off his hands in a day or so. If not, he could go to a mechanic or a body shop for something that would strip the skin raw.

That depended on how the next hour went.

Vo looked around, but couldn't find a blindfold and a cigarette. Just a towel for wiping his hands.

He steeled himself and climbed up onto the bed.

If you're gonna do it, do it right.

He straddled the backs of her legs and let his weight settle on his knees. He would cut off all the circulation to her feet if she had to hold him up.

The room was warm, but her back was all goose-pimply. Hopefully, she was as nervous about this as he was.

It took a second to figure out how to open the bottle, and then pour a good dollop on the exact spot between her shoulder blades.

This would probably fall under first aid training refresher, if anyone asked. He was certified as a medic. He could make that stretch.

The rest of the evening fell under PsyOps.

Identify your enemy, probe their weaknesses, exploit them.

At that level of psychology, pretty girls and Imperial ground commanders probably weren't that far apart, all things considered.

Vo let his brain go into a steady state, almost meditation. He worked the lotion into her soft skin with his own rough palms, using just enough force to grind her muscles loose, but not her bones. Less than he would have used with one of his marines. He didn't figure she was nearly as tough.

"You can work harder," she murmured. Or maybe purred. It was hard to differentiate the two. "I'm not made of porcelain."

Vo grunted something noncommittal and squeezed harder on the long muscles of her back. Crab claws pinching and pulling, back and forth. Up to her neck under that braid, down her back to her…

Crap.

…to her bottom.

Shut up and soldier, marine.

He slid backwards half a meter and began to work on possibly the finest bottom he had ever seen. Certainly ever touched. All muscle.

Down the left thigh first. Work the calf, the heel, the arch.

Crossover and work your way up the right in reverse order.

Come back down. Cross again. Back up the left.

Oh, what the hell.

Vo slid forward again and worked his way up her sides. Brushing against her breasts was simply unavoidable. Keep it firm. Keep it professional. Move on.

Up to the shoulders.

He had been afraid she was falling asleep on him. When he hit her right shoulder, she hissed in pain.

She started to rise, but he put more of his weight on her back and held her in place as he worked the muscles.

"It hurts," she whimpered.

"You worked twice as hard as most marines today, Phoebe," he replied softly. "Of course it hurts."

"Oh."

She subsided under his grip.

More lotion. More muscles. Down the right arm one muscle group at a time. Work the wrist, the palm. Back up the front. Across the neck. Down the left side. And up. Over the top of the shoulders, but keep her on her front.

Again.

Again.

Time passed. Vo meditated on all the sins he was committing in his head. He was almost finished.

"Do you want your scalp done?" he asked.

"Hmmm?"

He repeated himself.

"Yes, please," came the dreamy response.

Vo wiped as much lotion off as he could and attacked the string holding her braid, and then remembered all his survival skills untying it.

Getting her hair pulled softly but firmly seemed to be acceptable, to hear her purr.

Vo found himself done. And sweating. The exercise didn't explain it all.

He slid off the side of the bed, grabbed her robe, and draped it across her body.

That might have woken her, from the look on her face.

"So now what?" she inquired vaguely.

"I go home," Vo said. "You take a shower to wash the lotion out of your hair, and then soak for as long as you want, and then go to bed."

"You have to stay," she said firmly. "You promised me a glass of wine."

The PsyOps training, all that interrogation work, kept him from saying anything irrevocably stupid. At that point. He bit his tongue instead.

Her eyes got a teasing glint.

"You don't have to watch me take a bath, Vo," she smiled up at him. "You can find a game to watch. I promise to let you go home after a glass of wine, if you want."

Want. Really? What did want *have to do with it?*

"I'll find a book on your shelf," he countered. "There were a couple that looked interesting."

He turned and took three strides into the living room without looking back.

And breathed.

He found a half-stack of shelves, maybe a hundred titles in all. Actual ink on paper books. Expensive. He had left his computer at the apartment, and wasn't about to borrow one of hers. Not right now.

"Vo," Phoebe's voice got his attention.

He looked over from his squat. She had wrapped herself fully up in the robe and belted it. That was good.

The look on her face was vulnerable. Almost pained.

"Don't go?" she whispered.

"I'll be right here, Phoebe," he replied firmly, pulling a history of the early Republic with him as he stood.

Vo knew she was coming. Partly, he was that keyed up. Partly, the floor squeaked enough.

He had gotten four chapters into the book while he waited for her. It was pretty good. He might ask to borrow it, or buy his own copy.

He heard her let out a deep breath in relief from the door. Apparently, she hadn't been expecting him to still be here.

He looked up at her from the end of the big, comfy sofa closest to the fireplace.

She had gotten cleaned up, and relaxed. She was wearing baggy blue sweat pants and a green t-shirt, possibly with a sports bra underneath. Her long, brown hair was still a little damp and tied back in a simple tail.

She had stripped off all her makeup. He only noticed it by the absence.

"You stayed," she said softly with relief.

"Someone insisted I owed her a glass of wine," he smiled back.

"And you do," she said firmly as she moved past him. "Stay there. I'll be right back."

Rather than stare at her bottom, Vo stuck his nose back in his book and let his ears track her.

Into the kitchen. Grab an old-fashioned glass bottle off the rack. Open two drawers looking for the tool to remove the cork. Finally get it open. Locate two glasses. Pour. Cap the bottle with some sort of siphon pump. Return.

She was holding two faintly-blue goblets of a dark purple liquid when she returned. It was probably extremely expensive, very nice, and totally wasted on a guy like him. Like the rest of the joint.

Phoebe handed him a glass and retreated to the other end of the couch, curling her feet up under her in a way that reminded him of a ship's cat.

He took a sip. Yup, utterly wasted on his palate.

Vo wondered if he should learn to appreciate good wine. He had done the same thing when he first encountered proper coffee, after Command Centurion Keller had gotten everybody aboard *Auberon* hooked on the good stuff.

"Feeling better?" he asked as she settled in.

"An hour ago, I thought I would never move again," she replied with a groan. "Now I feel like I've slept all night and could do for a long run."

"Good," Vo said. "That means I did something right."

"You did lots of things right, Vo," she said with a warm smile as she took a sip of wine. Something changed in her eyes. "But you aren't staying, are you?"

He took a drink of the wine to order his thoughts. Reorder.

"Was it something I did?" she continued.

He could hear the emotion underneath her syllables. Nervousness, but tinged with pain. He might have never picked the word out, but the best way to describe her right now would be *fragile*. Like handling delicate glass.

Not exactly a task for a bull in a china shop.

"Nothing you did," he replied slowly.

"Something I didn't do?"

"No, it's not that either," Vo said.

The proper gentleman and big brother wanted to stop there. Leave it vague and ambiguous. Let things slide.

Something in her eyes drew him. The voice was off. The hands weren't right. The head was tilted the wrong way. The million little clues they teach you about interrogation technique were screaming at him.

He could almost see the indicators on the training tape. Look here. Watch this. Etc.

The wrongness almost soured the wine in his mouth.

"What?" Phoebe whispered.

"You make me nervous," Vo said, honestly.

She laughed. It was a trifle off. Nervous relief. Inappropriate for the situation.

"I make every man nervous," she replied, maybe with a touch of anger underneath.

He could see her shoulders come down a little. Those wonderful, long muscles in her back unknotted.

"No," Vo disagreed. "You intimidate them. That's different."

"And nothing intimidates you, Vo?" she asked quietly.

He shrugged. That was actually an entry in his personnel file. Navin the Black had showed it to him, once.

"Is there someone else?" Phoebe continued. "Another woman?"

Again, the shrug. No. She deserved more of an answer. It might make things easier. Maybe harder. At least cleaner. He already felt the need for a shower, himself.

"Kinda," he said quietly. "But I'm not sure she even knows I exist."

"Oh," Phoebe said. "That, I understand."

Vo was pretty sure the look of disbelief on his face was enough words.

"Vo, they see the boobs, or the butt, or the pretty face," Phoebe continued. "They see my parent's money, or their connections. If anyone ever looks at me, they see me as a means, or a notch on a bedpost. I honestly can't remember the last time I dealt with a gentleman."

Gentleman. Right. The thug from the streets of Anameleck Prime. What the hell am I doing here? Oh. Right. She still hasn't come clean. She's up to something, wants something. Has danced around it. Continues to dance.

He would just have to keep probing, keep pushing, until she came clean. Or his paranoia got the better of him.

The interrogator wanted to unravel her psyche. By now, he had a pretty good idea where her buttons were. Everyone had them. Not everyone realized it. Something to drive you to a sudden rage. Something to shatter you like a dropped glass. Something to make a pretty girl purr.

Vo felt like the greater of two evils. Any two evils. Pick one.

She was close to coming apart right now under unknown paired stresses, pulling her two opposite directions at once.

Vo had a lovely sword in his hands. And he couldn't bring himself to use it.

He settled for a shrug. There were no safe words at this moment.

"She's a fool," Phoebe said darkly.

Suddenly, she was close enough to touch. She reached out her left hand and just touched the back of the hand holding his suddenly-empty wine glass.

Where had the wine gone?

"Can I ask a favor?" she said softly.

Vo wondered if she had found his buttons. This was one he hadn't realized was there until now. Tomorrow, he would have to do something about it. Tomorrow.

"Sure," he replied, just as softly.

She was close enough to breathe on, but didn't have that look in her eyes like she wanted a kiss. There was a lot more pain when he looked. More than had been there before.

"Hold me?" she whispered.

He nodded.

With a shift, she was in his lap, curled up almost like a cat, with her head on his chest.

Carefully, he found the side table and set the empty wine glass down and then wrapped his arms around her. She was clean and lovely and warm. This much he could do.

She still hadn't told him anything.

The sound of the front door lock quietly surrendering brought Vo from dozing to combat-drop readiness in less than a heartbeat. Too many years on active duty. Trouble came in the dead of night. Marines who wanted to survive got there first.

He started to surge upright, realized he still had a sleeping cat of a girl on his lap, and twisted sideways to deposit her safely and softly on the couch. There wasn't anything heavy close, but he was confident enough in his unarmed combat skills to handle whoever would be sneaking in this late at night.

Sneaking?

He hadn't seen any evidence of a roommate. The other bedroom had been converted fully to an office. Hopefully, Phoebe hadn't forgotten to mention a boyfriend. It might get a bit touchy in here.

Vo was in the entry hallway, quickly, behind where the door would open, as silent as possible. Phoebe was stirring on the sofa, but not quite coherent yet. She had been deep.

The door opened. At least a little bit. Enough to see that the lights were still on in the living room.

"Phoebe?" a man's voice called quietly.

So, not a burglar. Or, at least not a stranger. Someone expecting her. Probably not expecting him. Vo stood perfectly still.

A man came into view. Short. Really short. Shorter than Phoebe. Pudgy. Bald but for a ring of gray hair around his skull. Vo would have said mousy, but the face reminded him of a vole.

He was dressed in corduroy pants and a tweed jacket, the kind with leather patches on the elbows that seemed to be a universal identification badge of a professor of social sciences. Vo wondered if they all shopped from the same catalog. The stranger carried a large leather briefcase in one hand.

"Phoebe?" he called louder.

In vino, veritas. In wine, you find truth.

Fear and surprise are also useful tools.

Vo reached out and pushed the door closed with a hard palm after the man entered. It made a satisfying thump as it slammed.

"Hiya," Vo smiled his best predator-in-the-night look.

The look on the vole's face was utterly priceless. It was almost a cartoon moment from his youth.

The tiny man turned, looked up in a total panic, and nearly wet himself cringing. He didn't say anything, but Vo was almost sure the intruder mouthed the word *Arlo* as he gasped and dropped the satchel in the middle of the hall.

Papers went everywhere when the latch failed.

Phoebe was finally awake enough to enter the fray. She appeared at the mouth of the hallway, hair slightly messed but otherwise finally back in the land of the living.

"Dr. Demir?" she asked in soft shock. "What are you doing here?"

The man ignored her. He had dropped to his knees and was frantically gathering pieces of paper up and sliding them back into the briefcase as fast as he could.

Vo couldn't move without stepping on something, so he stood perfectly still and watched the little man like a hawk. And, after a moment, Phoebe as well.

You never knew, with some folks. There were only so many ways to spin a situation like this when you were trying to do damage control.

Vo had learned a long time ago that if you tried to live your entire life aboveboard, you didn't have to spend any time trying to remember which lies you had told to what people. It was not a lesson many people ever seemed to learn. At least he could sleep nights with a clear conscience.

"I'm sorry, Phoebe," the little man, apparently a Doctor Demir, stammered. "I can explain."

Vo realized he could reach his boots without moving, and his butt was against the hall closet where his jacket was hanging. He pivoted enough to open the door and grab it, and then reached for his boots.

"Phoebe," he said softly, but with a warm smile. "I think this is my cue to leave. Thank you for a lovely day."

She started to say something, but Vo had the door open, slid through, and pulled it shut behind him. He could get to the ground floor via the fire stairs, and out into the night. The buses were still running, so he could get home and figure out what the hell had just happened.

III

Date of the Republic October 10, 394 Quinta City, Quinta

Even on a remote and kind-of backwater planet like *Quinta*, there were gossips. Vo hadn't expected mankind's better virtues to overwhelm their normal behavior, just because they had colonized the galaxy.

Quinta hadn't let him down.

If anything, being so far off the beaten path, so insular, worked to his benefit. A planet this remote wasn't constantly aping the styles and mannerisms of the more core worlds of the *Republic of Aquitaine*. Or, if they were, it was from decades or generations ago.

They tended to be more blinkered here. It was the kind of place where your great-grandchildren might still be called immigrants to their faces a century from now. People chattered like chickens, neighborhood style, rather than maintaining a big-city reticence.

With a little looking, you could find almost anything. You just needed to know how to ask the search programs.

Aeolus Demir, PhD. Fifty-three years standard. Tenured professor of political science, Quinta Colonial Institute. Expert in comparative political institutions with a specialization in the *Fribourg Empire*'s Planetary Governance systems. Nineteen papers published in peer-reviewed journals. Six books. Dry, boring, and technical. At least the three Vo had sampled with nothing better to do on a Sunday morning.

Never married. No scandals. Only 1.65 meters tall, so short, pudgy, balding.

And on good enough terms with the prettiest girl in school that he could let himself into her apartment very late on a Saturday night and she didn't scream or threaten to call the police.

While she happened to have the biggest rugby prop in school handy.

Interesting.

Vo had been expecting a boyfriend when a man's voice came through the open door. For no other reason than she was a pretty girl, he had been expecting someone tall and athletic. Lean. Probably blond. Someone like a younger version of Command Centurion Kigali off *CR-264*, except one that preferred girls.

A short, mousy, dumpy, middle-aged professor was just about the last thing he had expected.

And vice versa.

Except.

Arlo played the scene back in his head again. He would be willing to put money that Demir had recognized him.

Which made no sense, since he didn't have a class with the man, and had only been on planet a little over eight weeks.

And Phoebe's response hadn't rung the right bells at the time, but he had been gone, maybe a little too quickly, to follow up.

She hadn't been surprised that the man could get in, only that he was there late on a Saturday night without calling first.

What would Phoebe see in a man like that?

He flashed back to her on the sofa. Lovely, and warm, and vulnerable. Under the eye of a trained interrogator already keyed up.

What had she said?

"If anyone ever looks at me, they see me as a means, or a notch on a bedpost. I honestly can't remember the last time I dealt with a gentleman."

So let's assume the relationship between them isn't physical. She could have any man in school, just by batting her eyelashes.

Vo blushed.

Almost any man.

Still.

Maybe it isn't what she wanted from Demir, but something the little professor wanted from her? A means?

What could he offer to a pretty girl with her parent's connections and wealth?

Excitement? Phoebe didn't strike him as a rush-junky-type, like some of his marines frequently were, until they got that knocked out of them by one of the Yeomen or Centurions.

She didn't need money. Her parents were loaded and that flat had cost more to decorate than he made last year.

He doubted a physical relationship.

And Demir obviously hadn't registered on Phoebe as a gentleman, so whatever they had wasn't a particularly nice relationship.

Did he have something on her?

Vo's brain clicked so hard it nearly hurt. It had that same implacable feeling as the locks on a howitzer dropping into place, just before you pulled the lanyard and belched death skyward.

If she was being compelled by someone, someone with something dark and extremely embarrassing on her, most of her behavior suddenly made a lot more sense.

So, you have something to blackmail the prettiest girl in school. Throw this pretty girl at the dumb marine. Have her convince him to do something stupid, to impress said pretty girl. Most marines would, especially for a pretty girl. Suborn said dumb marine. Blackmail him. Blackmail them both.

Every bad thriller Vo had ever read rolled out of the darkness and laughed at him right now. Every bad computer gaming fantasy, where he got to save the galaxy as the big, damn hero. Everything.

And yet…

Vo reached back to the ancient classics, literature that predated starflight, and would outlive empires. A man had once said that once you eliminated everything else, whatever remains, no matter how strange, must be the truth.

Nothing else made a damned lick of sense.

For a moment, the evil conscience on his left shoulder nearly won out.

It would be remarkably easy to contact the appropriate authorities on this world and whisper the correct specific key words into the right paranoid ears. On *Auberon*, he had spent the last three years being those ears.

They would quietly round up the mousy little professor and disappear him into the deepest hole imaginable, while they dismantled his entire existence to look for crimes. The little gremlin on his shoulder smiled.

Nobody was as pure as the driven snow. Nobody.

Once the authorities started looking, they would find something. Everybody had secrets. If the *Fribourg Empire* didn't own him already, Republic Intelligence would when they were done with Dr. Demir.

That kind of power was dangerous.

The good conscience on his right shoulder looked remarkably like a six-centimeter-tall ogre version of Navin the Black. Senior Centurion Crncevic, *Auberon's* Dragoon. His boss.

The ogre just cleared his throat and raised an eyebrow at Vo.

There was a pretty girl who would be sucked up by such an investigation. She would never get away from those kinds of people, either. Then she would discover what a small fish she really was.

Had she done anything at all to warrant being disappeared into a small gray box, besides try to flirt with a man whose job entailed professional paranoia?

Vo wrestled back and forth for nearly an hour before he gave up. The risk/reward ratio just didn't justify bringing the big guns to the party. And she hadn't done anything to piss him off that much.

It was all speculation on his part. Occupational hazard.

He was just about finished fixing his lunch when the doorbell rang.

It was probably automatic that his hand reached out and touched the block of wood with all his kitchen knives in handmade slots. His brain wasn't really that deep in the dark and foreboding places, right?

The soup was done. He turned the heat off and left his sandwich on the counter.

It was all of four steps to the door. He hadn't bothered to bring any firearms with him to this planet, which was good, or one would be in his hand right now. The cricket paddle by the door was within easy reach, and easy enough to explain, if someone had ever come into his apartment.

Vo took a deep breathe peeked through the hole.

The girl. Alone.

Really, Vo? The Girl? Phoebe, man. Innocent until proven guilty, right?

Vo unlocked the door and opened it partway, leaning innocently against it in such a way that anchored it in place as surely as concrete.

"Hi," he smiled down at her, feeling like one of the ogres on his shoulder. Left or right would depend on the rest of the conversation.

Combat-mode he couldn't help, but he could at least be polite. He was way too keyed up to be especially warm and friendly right now.

Phoebe had a fragile smile pasted on her face.

"I wanted to apologize for last night," she stammered up at him.

Vo couldn't help himself. He leaned forward enough to look past her out the door before he stepped back. This was not a conversation to have with his neighbors around.

Not that they had been nosy, but still.

"Come in," he said. "Just about to sit down to lunch. Can I make you something?"

He moved out of her way and she came past him.

He glanced once out the door again and then closed and locked it before turning his attention to the girl.

Vo enjoyed the way she climbed out of her jacket and handed it to him. She was a seriously distracting woman, regardless of everything else.

He hung her coat on a hook next to his jacket. Her perfume still reminded him of arboreal forests.

"Thank you, Vo," she smiled carefully up at him. "I don't think I could eat right now."

It was probably the paranoia speaking, but he hadn't told her where he lived. Even Finn didn't know, unless the man had quietly followed him home after class sometime. And he didn't have any reason to.

A week ago, Vo might not have noticed such a tail.

Today was an entirely different matter.

He pulled out the second chair to his tiny dining table and seated her correctly. At least the Fleet made Marines take classes in deportment.

"Some lemonade?" he asked as he moved into the tiny kitchen part and let his reflexes organize the soup, ladle in the drawer, bowls in the left-hand cupboard.

"Thank you, Vo," Phoebe replied. "That would be lovely."

Grab two mismatched plastic cups, reach into the well-stocked fridge for the lemonade jug, pour, set on the table. Grab the soup bowl and a spoon, bring the sandwich.

Take the other chair.

Smile at her and take a sip of soup.

Pawn to King's Four, White.

The ancient board game of Chess wasn't his thing. It was something the Dragoon had been trying to teach him. Jackson Tawfeek was all over it, might even be a grandmaster one of these days, but not Vo.

Vo was happy just to learn.

To be any good at the game, you had to get inside your opponent's head and calculate several response ahead. Here, Vo thought he was making headway. As sneaky as the girl across from him might be, he was playing a much meaner game than he had yesterday.

Higher stakes. Rougher rules.

She seemed to have been prepared for that. Instead of dressing in something tight that showed her figure off in distracting ways, she was in a baggy sweater and loose pants.

Girlie, but today not a girl to write home about. If he were ever to write home about a girl. And it wouldn't be this one, anyway.

Probably.

Vo took a bite of sandwich and chewed.

Normally, he inhaled something like this with no more thought than consuming the requisite amount of calories to keep in shape and not turn into a lardball.

Today, he chewed slowly, deliberately, staring at her as he did with a goofy grin.

She sipped her lemonade and stared back at him intently with a soft, slightly-uncertain smile.

Pawn to King's Four, Black. A mirror move that gave nothing away.

Vo had more props, as well as home pitch advantage. He grabbed the spoon and took a sip from the soup. It wasn't from true scratch, but it also wasn't dumped out of a can and reheated. It just happened that he was frugal enough to make broth from chicken bones left over from other meals, plus whatever bag of frozen vegetables was on sale at the grocery.

And the soup was pretty good. Vo smiled at her and took another sip. He had never hunted elk. He had, however, been in the bush after more dangerous game than pretty girls.

If there was anything more dangerous.

Another bite of sandwich. Chew carefully and try not to spill anything down your front as you do.

Her patience ran out before his food did.

"I'm not going to outwait you, am I, Vo?" she finally asked.

"I can make you a sandwich if you're hungry," he volleyed back. It was a warm smile. Home pitch advantage meant he could be friendly. She hadn't done or said anything yet to warrant him playing truly mean. Not that it would be a bright idea, right now, but you never knew with some people.

"Most men would be jealous, or angry, or defensive right now," she plowed ahead, apparently working from a script in her head. She sounded like she was trying to convince herself as much as him.

"Why?" he replied evenly, possibly even innocently.

The interrogator came to the fore and began to measure her eyes and hands. She was good, but would never be a professional gambler. Plus, he had a handle on her buttons if he needed to push.

"Last night," she said with a vague hand wave, as if that explained it all.

Vo took another bite of his sandwich. Who knew that bologna and Swiss cheese with a little mustard would be such a useful defensive weapon?

Knight to Queen's Bishop Three, White.

"You had unexpected company," he said with as much innocence as he could muster into his words. "It seemed like a fortuitous time to depart."

"Don't you want to know what was going on?" she asked, prying at his defenses, trying to draw him into moving a bishop.

Pawn to Queen's Three, Black.

Time to push a button.

"Phoebe," Vo replied calmly, as nonchalantly as he could modulate his voice. "It's none of my business. I shouldn't have been there that late, but you fell asleep and I didn't want to wake you up."

"You made me feel safe," she said after a beat, very quietly.

Fragile was in her voice again.

Vo wondered how much of it was real, and how much was a role she was playing.

Push hard.

Midgame was always where Tawfeek suddenly expressed his genius on the board. Vo found chess too strictly limiting. There were only so many things you could do, and only so many ways to do them. Ops in the field were never that clean.

Maybe that was why he was a better marine than chess player.

Pawn to King's Rook Four, White.

"I don't belong there," he said simply.

He was rewarded by a sudden blink and a slight flush to her skin. She leaned back and stared at the horizon, eyes flickering back and forth.

Internally, Vo smiled. The next words out of her mouth were likely to be a wonderful helping of lies, whatever she said. She was pretty fast in assembling her response, as far off track as he had driven her from her script.

But he was watching her like a hawk.

Externally, he took another innocent bite of his sandwich.

"Why not?" she finally said defensively, a beat too late to be an honest response.

Pawn to Queen's Four, Black.

At least he didn't feel like the greater of two evils for his thoughts about the girl anymore.

Knight to King's Three, White.

"You're money, Phoebe," he added with a soft sneer, sounding as much as he could like the seventeen-year-old punk who ran away from the slums of Anameleck Prime to become a marine.

Once upon a lifetime ago.

"I'm a mutt from the streets with no money, no connections, and another couple of decades on the line ahead of me before I can retire and make a go of the private sector. I am most definitely not your type, lady."

Nine times in ten, he would get the lemonade in his face right now, followed by her stomping out the front door, slamming it hard in his face, and never talking to him again. That was the honest response to his tone and his words.

Life was not a romance novel, regardless of what his littlest sister might believe. Sonja read too much of that crap, anyway.

Maybe Phoebe did, too. She had completely lost the script in her head.

For once, both the consciences on his shoulders agreed, if for very different reasons.

"You were a perfect gentleman last night, Vo," she flailed.

"And you knew that when you decided to get almost completely naked in front of me and let me have my way with you? Or when you went to take a bath and left me in the living room? Or feel asleep in my lap?"

Vo let the anger he had been tamping down rumble a little at this point. Not much, just enough to stir the cauldron some more. He wanted her to stay off balance.

"I already knew that…" she started to say.

"And why was Dr. Demir coming to your flat so late?"

Knock her mentally sideways. Hard. Like he had been taught.

"He wanted to find out about…"

She clammed up before the damning words were actually spoken, but they were there in her eyes, along with fear.

But she wasn't afraid of him. No, not good old Vojciech Arlo, hero of the *Republic of Aquitaine* Navy.

At least, not enough.

He watched her set the cup down deliberately, when he could tell she really did want to throw it in his face, but not for the obvious reasons. She slid her chair back and stood quickly.

Vo moved quickly as well, standing and stepping back.

She made it to the door in five steps and started to pull it open.

He put all of his weight behind slamming it shut again. It made a rewarding thump that rattled the whole building.

Vo turned and looked down at her as she suddenly cowered in front of him. He barely restrained the snarl that wanted to come out and play right now. His breath was heavy with menace.

She actually started to shrink, sliding along the wall and back a little, finding a corner where the wall jutted out slightly.

He was back to being the greater of any two evils again, at least in his own head.

It took everything he had not to clench and unclench his fists as he watched her. This woman, this rich, little girl, with absolutely every advantage he had never had, she had wanted to play him. Play with him. Something.

He might finally be ready to be angry.

Probably the only honest response he had gotten from her so far was the relief that he hadn't snuck quietly out while she was in her bath.

Hadn't wriggled off the hook.

"Do you want to finally tell me the truth, Phoebe?" he ground out over clenched teeth.

"I can't," she whispered, trapped and on the verge of panic.

That sounded close to a truth. She was beginning to fear him almost as much as she did whoever else it was that had such a grip on her soul.

"Why not?" he continued, leaning in close and looking over her.

Push the button. Firmly but relentlessly. Height, mass, and the implied risk of brutality were useful tools for a big man, especially against a woman. Not one of his female marines, like First Rate Spacer Nadine Orly, but effective against a civilian like this pretty girl.

Orly would kick him in the balls right now. Phoebe didn't think like that.

Her breath started to come in sharp, shallow gasps.

Adrenaline was an utter bitch. Part of marine basic was learning to master that sudden spike of power and fear. Some people froze, others puked. But the rest learned to cope, made it a tool.

Or, in his case, spent years under the watchful eye of Navin the Black honing it to a fine, killing edge.

Vo didn't need her blood on the floor right now, physically or metaphorically.

"I'm waiting, Phoebe," he snarled quietly. It was almost a growl.

She flinched.

"I can't," she repeated in a tiny whisper.

"Who are you afraid of, Phoebe?" he pressed.

Use the target's name. Repeat it. It becomes an icepick stabbing them in the brain, every time they hear it. Wear them down like water dropping on rocks.

Slowly. Implacably.

"They'll…"

She shut herself down again. She wouldn't give *them* up. Not yet.

But he was close to breaking through.

"Phoebe," he said calmly, letting the menace drain out and replacing it with some modicum of reassurance. "I can protect you from Demir."

"No," she whispered. "Nobody could protect me from him. Nobody can save me."

The pain was back in her eyes. The fragility. The impossible depths of darkness.

Success, if you wanted to call it that.

Vo had seen the signs before. The girl was in shock. Serious psychological trauma. World-ending stuff. The brain goes into either hyperdrive or shuts down completely.

He reached out and put a hand on her shoulder, curled it around her shoulder blade, tugged against her rigid posture. Pushing someone that hard, that far, in an interrogation was second nature now.

That's when the truth usually came out.

"I'm a marine, Phoebe," he said, trying to pour strength into her from the touch. "The *Republic of Aquitaine* Navy. The good guys."

"Oh, Vo," she said, relaxing and finally leaning into him.

He felt her arms wrap around his waist as she tried to press herself flat against his stomach. He let his long arms encompass her.

After a moment, she leaned back and looked up at him. He could see tears wanting to fall, but holding at the corners of her eyes.

"Do you think it's possible?" she asked.

"I'm sorry about everything, Phoebe," he replied quietly. "But I needed to get through to you."

"Thank you."

She leaned forward again, turning her head to the side, as if listening to his heart rate. It wouldn't be normal right now.

"Who do you know who can help?" she continued.

Something was still off in her voice. Interrogator caught it, pointed it out.

Every interrogation was different, but every one ended up on the same spectrum, that same line from right to left. And she wasn't on it. Or rather, she was clear out on the right end of the scale, looking down off a cliff.

Out where normal people never landed. Out with the card sharps and the grifters. Out in a place where they used to call them psychopaths. Human on the outside, but lacking the full range of natural emotions inside. Badly wired, they had to mimic how they saw other humans act.

And there was always a lag, a subtle moment when that kind of person had to figure out what the normal response would be, the human response, calculate it, and then enact it.

Most people would never catch them. You had to be keyed up, paranoid, and watching. Or in this case, have her pressed up against you where you could feel the play of her muscles in her back as she thought and moved.

Hopefully, his own heart hadn't just given him away. He could always tell her it was the emotion of the moment, of being able to help a pretty girl.

It would make a useful lie.

"I'm not sure," he replied, letting his own emotions jangle his tones. "But I'm sure I'll be able to think of something. Pretty girls should always be rescued from dragons, as my auntie used to say."

"Oh, Vo," she repeated, almost breathless. "I knew I could count on you. So now what?"

Quicksand had that same queasy feel to it. Sand sitting on water, floating like a solid, until you put any weight on it and sank. Thrashing just sucked you deeper.

"I need to think," he said, honestly enough. "You go home. Tomorrow after class, we'll go somewhere and talk."

"Thank you, Vo," she hugged him tightly, pressing her breasts flat against his stomach muscles again.

Phoebe let go quickly and turned, almost inside his arms. Vo managed to withdraw his hands before he ended up cupping her breasts, as much as he wanted to.

She glanced over her shoulder at him with a grin and a wink, and pulled her jacket off the hook.

Vo watched as she made a scene of turning to face him and climbing back into her coat, stretching like a cat as she did.

He stood perfectly still, a mouse with an owl somewhere overhead.

She stepped close and gestured. Vo leaned down far enough for a quick, warm kiss on the lips.

"See you tomorrow, handsome," she said, reaching for the door, opening it, and disappearing as it closed.

Most of the marines he had ever known would be blind with lust right now. She seemed to be counting on that.

Vo could think of sixteen times he had been present in a serious interrogation or studied it afterwards for class. The nasty ones, when it was necessary to push someone to the breaking point using the whole range of emotional and psychological tools. Average recovery time, according to experience and literature, fifteen to twenty minutes. Even adrenaline took a while to break down.

Not thirty seconds.

Everything, even the hug, had been a lie.

For a moment, the left-hand ogre almost won the argument.

Make the call, feed her to the ravenous beast that was Republic Intelligence, get on with his life.

The right-hand ogre kicked him in the ear.

"By the book, punk," he could hear Navin the Black growl at him. "It exists for a reason. Use it. Understand it. Master it. Then we'll talk."

Vo stared at Phoebe, walking away, through the closed door.

He was finally angry.

Vo's soup had turned to ashes in his mouth. Or perhaps cardboard. Morning oatmeal with nothing on top except rage.

He finished it anyway and automatically cleaned everything into the sink, including her half-glass of lemonade. That got poured away.

He had exactly one day to endgame this. He wasn't nearly good enough to pull off any sort of con against a professional like Phoebe for long. She was too much like his ex-brother-in-law, Karol, Zorana's very-short-term first husband that nobody in the family had much liked, or missed.

In twenty-four hours, he would either have to walk away, or make a call that ended up possibly destroying her life, and several other people around her.

On a hunch.

Well-trained. Well experienced. Professional.

But still a hunch.

What the hell did Demir have on her that could hold a woman that smart on a leash that tight? *Quinta* wasn't a particularly puritanical place about women, not like most of the *Fribourg Empire*, so any youthful indiscretions shouldn't be that bad.

You had to work hard for the judge to offer you immediate enlistment in the marines instead of six-to-nine months in the pokey. Really hard.

Something else he understood, probably far better than the girl did.

So, the fussy little professor had something on the girl. And it was good. And she couldn't destroy it to free herself, either because she didn't know where it was, or it was secured so well she couldn't get at it.

Vo sat at the tiny kitchen table for two and visualized the game board.

Chess has two colors. Again, one of its major failings, to a marine used to ten thousand options he could use to achieve success, from orbital strikes to spider mines.

He had been playing white.

Time to switch sides.

Black King has a hold on Black Queen.

She can spill her secrets to a white horse who wandered up, if she dared.

She doesn't dare.

She might be free, if the dragon's loot could be stolen. Or even destroyed in a fire.

So we assume the dragon won't store it in his house, where a terrible accident might happen.

Plus, if it is that important, he would want to keep closer watch on it. Keep it handy, keep it…

Vo felt his heart sink.

A satchel of papers. One that Demir dropped when someone scared him. And that he was more concerned about gathering it all up than he was about being mugged by the big, scary marine, or explaining to the girl why he was in her flat in the dead of night.

Important papers, too, and not just the random mish-mash of student assignments on fourteen different colors of paper, or a latest manuscript that would be all in one big folder, or research that would be a random collection of news-clippings, static copies, and printouts.

Everything that had fallen had looked well-organized, professional. The sorts of files Navin the Black kept.

Personnel files.

Crap.

Was I looking at my own file in that mess? Could I have reached down, picked it up, and unraveled everything accidentally? Would I have even realized it?

If life wasn't one of Sonja's romance novels, it wasn't one of his mystery thrillers either, even the cozy ones. X never marked the spot, and old Farmer Johnson wasn't the guy under the monster mask.

Maybe.

Tomorrow, Dr. Demir would probably be very, very cautious, while he waited on what Phoebe learned from her big, dumb, marine hero after class. He couldn't be randomly mugged. If the professor had any sense, the satchel could be destroyed, but the originals of the files would be secured in a bank vault somewhere, with only the copies of the information close at hand.

Vo would need to access the satchel secretly. Read the contents.

Dead of night.

Black bag job.

Cat-burglary. Breaking and entering. Armed trespass. Theft of private property. Possession of stolen goods.

The sorts of things that get sealed in a court file when a Minor accepts the Court's offer to run away and become a Marine, and therefore, *Someone Else's Problem.*

Vo popped the bones in his neck and grimaced at the memory.

He had just spent eight years becoming a respectable member of society.

Respectable enough.

Was he really going to do something so stupid as to break into the guy's house?

Both consciences just shook their heads at him.

At least he had learned the arts of sneakiness and misdirection from one of the most dangerous men in the fleet.

Navin the Black.

IV

Date of the Republic October 11, 394 Quinta City, Quinta

It was dark on this street, but Vo could see well enough. It was one of those wonderful, upper-middle-class neighborhoods that seem to accumulate close to well-financed universities, in this case taking up one whole side of the campus, while the other three filled up with cheap student housing, bars, and restaurants.

Wide, tree-lined streets, with the trees just now starting to think about browning and dropping their leaves. Soft, grass-filled yards, well-manicured and landscaped. It would be quiet, unless a wind came up, and then the leaves would rustle all by themselves.

You didn't wear dead black for something like this. That was the mistake amateurs made, usually after watching too many ninja movies.

A black lump stood out. A mix of moderate grays actually blended better, especially against landscaping and bushes.

There would be lights on porches, and maybe motion sensors in back yards. People in a neighborhood like this would have cute little marker lights for walkways, like *Auberon*'s flight deck did for landing her dangerous little hawks.

It would be impossible to come at the place over the roofline. That only worked in slums, anyway.

Fortunately, there wouldn't be any feral dogs, either. Place like this would bring the family mutt in at night to guard the house, and keep them out of the weather.

Vo had a thing about dogs.

It had been a twenty minute walk from his apartment. And two whole socio-economic strata. Nice blue collar to genteel poverty.

These were old houses, starting to go to seed. The kinds of places professors in jackets with patches on the elbows would move into when they got tenure, keep for thirty or fifty years, and then sell when they retired.

Not many kids. No big party animals.

Quiet.

Seventeen-year-old Vo wondered if these morons even bothered to lock their doors at night. It had that kind of feel.

A candy store waiting for an urchin.

Grown-up Vo had spent several hours virtually touring the neighborhood on his computer, and then arranging all the supplies he thought he might need for a job like this.

He did miss the old tool-bag.

He could make do.

Vo had briefly considered blowing the closest transformer and blacking out the entire neighborhood for a few hours. That would get him past any alarms, but it would also probably wake people up and they might notice a ghost passing through their back alley.

Better to let them sleep.

Dr. Aeolus Demir. Bachelor. Tenured professor. Living in a monstrous, old, brick and wood house. Three stories above ground. Daylight windows indicating a basement below. A stupendous waste of living space, dedicated to housing just one man.

On *Anameleck Prime*, they would have sub-divided the joint and put at least eight families in there. Maybe ten. Vo only grumbled a little.

None of the publicity photos of the little doctor had indicated a dog. Not that it ruled it out, but it meant to plan for the possibility, and not the certainty.

Dogs don't like being zapped with a taze-charge any more than people do, and usually weigh a whole bunch less, so they get dropped harder. Vo wasn't taking any chances on getting bit tonight.

He had a thing about dogs.

Vo had sat perfectly still long enough that squirrels would have climbed up on his shoulders to look around by now, if there were any out this late. Maybe he'd get lucky and an owl would land on him soon.

There had been motions lights in the alley, two houses down. They had automatically gone dark again nearly forty-five minutes ago. Nobody had come out to look around.

Dr. Demir's house had a short staircase up to the back porch door, with a dim light over it that was just enough to illuminate the stairs. He presumed a laundry or mudroom beyond it. Some utter waste of useful space.

To the left, a darker spot indicated a set of steps down. The basement was barely half a deck down from the ground, maybe only a meter and a half. The door there was not lit, but he wasn't about to touch it. That would be the one door alarmed, even if nothing else was.

Not that he would have stopped at one, but he would have started there while he worked out the rest of the house. But then again, he was professionally paranoid.

How twitchy was the professor?

On the right was his target. An ancient, steep staircase, made from honest-to-goodness wood beams thicker than his forearms. Up one flight to a second story door, then up again to the third level.

Vo wondered now if the place had ever been sub-divided, and the professor hadn't bothered with that level of external remodel when he turned it back into a single-person mansion. It had that feel. Seedy, but recovered, like an alcoholic who has seen the light.

Those doors would be locked. Possibly alarmed. Hopefully not walled over inside.

At least they both had windows in the doors themselves.

It was late enough. If he moved now, he would have thirty minutes inside to work. If something happened at that point, he could hit the ground running, and hopefully get lost in whatever crowd of pedestrians were being chased out of the college bars when they closed on a Sunday night.

A slim hope, but better than being the only person on the street if the cops came sniffing.

Not that he had ever done something like this before, right?

Vo stirred. He looked left, right, back, forward.

Nothing but dark windows facing him. Hopefully without even-more-patient hunters in them.

One way to find out. At least he could always make that one call to the right people, if this blew up in his face.

It was a small soul. Cold and mean. But he liked it.

Vo pulled a scarf around the lower part of his face, took a breath, and moved...

Four steady strides across the alley way, Vo. From vine-covered wall to bushes besides an ancient outbuilding garage. You always move slowly, deliberately. Sudden movement draws the eye. Smooth blends.

Stop. Breathe. Listen. Calm.

Study the back windows here, looking for movement, reflection, lights.

Nothing.

Wait.

Nothing.

Ooze down the side of the building glacially. Become the last bush in the line.

Gargoyle.

Say a small prayer to Bes, the patron saint of cats. Cross the three meters of opening to the bottom of the stairs.

Step to the far right on each tread slowly. Do not cause the edifice to sway, buckle, or creak under your weight and movement.

Place each foot deliberately. You cannot explain why you are here, so you must be prepared to jump clear suddenly and run like hell.

Ignore the squeaking of the steps. Nobody inside should respond to noise, as long as you move patiently and don't rattle the building.

First landing. Look at the rear windows halfway below you as you make the turn.

Nothing.

Continue another half-flight to face the second-story door on an oversized balcony.

Mostly darkness inside behind drapes. Probably a room. Not walled over.

Breathe once. Attack the next set of steps.

Calm. Deliberate. You can leap from this height onto the grass and land safely. You qualified at Jump School from a higher elevation. Keep that in mind.

Make the turn, study the whole back of the building.

Still dark. Still quiet. Still waters.

Approach the third-story landing, barely a meter square. There is no light up here over the door, or it is turned off.

Explosion of sound as something moves, rushing right at your face and over your shoulder.

Crow. Angry at being chased out of his nest by a predator.

Breathe. Calm. Patience.

You have brought a flash, but do not use it yet.

Instead, study the window. Note the dust on the glass. Evidence of neglect. Hopefully, nobody uses this floor any more, except as storage and for parties.

Study the frame. Look for wires and plates.

There.

Someone has wired the door for a circuit alarm. Two pieces of metal rub lightly when the door is closed. They did a half-ass job of installing it, putting it inside the doorframe instead of inside the house where it would be invisible until opened. The circuit will break when someone opens the door more than a few centimeters. An alarm will sound.

You expected this.

Reach into the bag and pull out a two-meter length of wire with gator clips at both ends. Bring the small knife as well. Carve a very small moat in the wood next to both pieces of metal.

Clip the gators carefully.

Study the door. Do not touch it.

Old fashioned mechanical round handle that take a simple tumbler key. You no longer own dedicated lock-picks, but were able to improvise this afternoon. Muscle memory.

Slip the first piece of metal in. Turn the lock just enough to create tension. You cannot wear gloves tonight because you need the sensitivity.

Do not leave fingerprints anywhere until you can get the gloves out of your pocket.

Insert the probe next. Assume a standard design. Four vertical pins. Older than starflight. Good enough to stop anyone without some level of training, patience, and need.

Tickle the lock pins. Feel them release like the individual buttons down the front of your girlfriend's shirt as she slowly gives in.

Hold the torsion with care. Time is not critical, but important. Let's only do this once.

Feel that last pin surrender. Your girlfriend smiles up as she offers you the greatest birthday present a sixteen-year-old boy could ever imagine.

The lock turns slowly under your hand. Feel the mechanism give way. Turn the handle with slow care.

Glacial.

The latch lets go. Add the slightest bit of forward pressure, looking for a dead-bolt. Nothing.

Darkness.

Vo pushed the door open far enough to peek in and listen. At least no alarms filled the night.

So far, so good.

He slid sideways and shifted his head around to look at the back of the door. No secondary alarms or devices.

He listened to the building as he put away the picks and put on thin gloves. No voices, nor footsteps. Nothing to indicate awareness of an intruder, and the old building creaked anyway. Not much, but it hadn't been rebuilt to be rock solid inside. He would hopefully hear someone on the stairs.

Vo checked the gator clips, made sure they were solid, and moved away from the door, closing it almost, but leaving a space where he could pull it suddenly if running.

He stayed close to the left hand wall, away from the floor vent he could see, and not out in the middle where the old beams might squeak the most.

Each step was like gliding on ice now. He tried to become one with the house.

The roof pitched in steep here. The other end of the hall was a lovely stained glass design that should be centered over the front porch. Four doors faced each other in pairs, plus a spot where the stairwell opened on his left.

Vo pulled his flash now and turned it on just long enough to confirm the hallway.

There was some dust on the floor. Not much, but he would leave a trail of foot prints when he left, like on a snowy winter morning.

But it also eliminated this floor as a hiding spot.

He moved just far enough to peek down the stairs. Down a half flight it turned to the right and disappeared.

Again, darkness.

He stayed on the outside as he took each step slowly. The building squeaked and groaned with age and temperature-differential settling. Hopefully, nobody was watching him, evil-villain-style on a secret camera monitor.

He got to the first landing, peeked again.

Another half flight and it opened out onto a carpeted floor.

This level had nightlights plugged into the sockets in a couple of places, from the amount of ambient light. A resident would be able to navigate to the bathroom and back without having to turn anything on or bumping into something.

It was still silent. Hopefully, a good sign.

Vo crouched down and looked, and then crept forward when he didn't see anything.

This hallway was wider than the one above. There was space for an overstuffed chair to the left and a small bookcase to the right.

With a house like this, Vo assumed money. There were closed double doors at the end to the right, the back of the house. Hopefully, Demir didn't have to sleep with the satchel chained to his wrist, like that guy in that one spy-thriller movie.

Then it might be worth just taze-zapping him, tying him up, blindfolding him, and saying to hell with subtlety. That kind of situation would probably be evidence enough, anyway.

Speaking of.

Vo pulled the taze-pistol he had just bought today from his pocket and checked everything. Never assume the gun still works. He kept it in his left hand, low to his side. He could shoot with either hand at this range, and generally needed his right free to work.

Across and to his left was obviously the upstairs guest bathroom. He could see a nightlight brightening it up enough for strangers.

Vo assumed that the doors on the left would then be bedrooms. Would the two on the right be a library and an office? Demir could waste enough space to do that.

If not, I'll look downstairs. If all else fails, maybe we'll go for the strong-arm tactics.

He moved to his right, staying close to the wall. Both doors were cracked halfway open. Both rooms were dark.

There was a smell out of place here, but he couldn't identify it.

Barely a taste on the tip of his tongue. Sweet-sour. Not fresh flowers, or not anything he could place. Chemical. Faint.

The bottom edge of the double-door at the end was dark. Hopefully that meant that Demir had gone to sleep at a reasonable hour for Monday morning classes.

Vo would feel stupid doing all this breaking and entering, to not find the man at home.

He pulled the flashlight out of his pocket again and leaned into the first open doorway.

Nothing moved, so nothing got shot on reflex.

Vo had a thing about dogs.

He palmed the flashlight and flicked it on/off, on/off. The human eye does a wonderful job of retaining a sudden image. It was what made movies possible, where a still image flickered seventy-two times per second.

Library. Research style. Heavy on big books. The leather-bound kind that libraries and college professors preferred. Couple of talking chairs and a side table. Everything well organized.

Clean.

Nothing on the floor like a satchel. Or a dog.

Vo stopped and breathed.

Seriously, there wasn't any smarter way to do this?

He shrugged to himself and his twin consciences, and rotated in place.

He moved steadily across the carpet with his weight. Smooth, deliberate strides to the other side.

Darkness.

Again with the flashlight, on/off, on/off.

Office.

Workspace.

Messy.

Piles of books, papers, crap. File cabinet that looked serious. Knick-knacks you accumulate in your private space. Personal trophies. Leftovers. Swag.

Desk on the right with a chair.

Vo stepped into the room, past the half-open door, and pushed it to the frame, but not closed.

There was a window, but he didn't want to have to Tarzan his way out, or worse, through it. That was a good way to break a leg.

Three steps in, he struck paydirt. Maybe.

The satchel. A satchel. Hopefully the only satchel.

Next to the chair, just beyond, almost hidden from sight. About where you would drop it if you had just collapsed into the chair.

Vo took two quick steps and leaned over to look. He did not touch.

It looked like the same satchel. The top was open. Eight centimeters of file folders inside, old school paper and binder clips.

That made sense. Anything not electronic was nothing that could be accessed, except by someone as willing to be here as he was.

Anyone willing to black-bag a place like this probably already knew what they would find, but electronic files were different.

Those had to be stored somewhere, transmitted across someone else's networks, were subject to random intercept by the sorts of smart filtering systems that Security folks played with. Not old-school *Sentiences*, like Suvi had been, but pushing right up against the limit of what Republic law would allow.

He fidgeted for a second, before putting the flashlight in his mouth and turning it on. Putting down the taze-pistol seemed like a dumb idea, and he needed a hand free to work.

Vo lifted the bag and set it on the chair. The flashlight tasted like wet dog, but that was probably just him sweating all over the cheap plastic earlier, and not any feeling of impending doom.

Nothing like that.

One meaty paw pulled out the thick stack of papers and carefully laid them flat on the desk.

He shifted his head so the light centered the pile.

It was already bad.

Arlo, Vojciech. Yeoman, RAN. Anameleck Prime.

And that was just the top folder.

He set the flashlight down where it cast a good reflection on the space and got to work.

Vo flipped the folder open and looked at a copy of the paperwork he had submitted when he enrolled at Quinta Colonial Institute. Under that, character reference letters from Navin the Black and Command Centurion Jessica Keller.

Wow? They really said that? About me?

Past that, notes of his class schedule, family, upbringing, and psychological profile. Everything anyone might want to know about the man that was public record, or easily accessible.

And a few things that weren't.

Nothing about sealed Court records from stupid youthful errors. Small wonders.

Vo felt his teeth start to grind, stopped them.

You knew this already, Arlo. This is confirmation. Now you can hopefully rescue the girl. Where's her file?

There were six more folders under his. He closed his up, put it to one side, and started to look at the next one. The name was nobody he knew.

The door to the room had opened silently.

He was face-down in papers and had lost track of his space.

The overhead light coming on blinded him, physically, mentally, and metaphorically.

"Do not move," a woman's voice snarled harshly at him. "Vo?"

His body froze. His brain went into overdrive.

Phoebe?

Vo tuned his head very slowly.

She was standing in the doorway, wearing something his brain called a linen shift, a word dredged up from whatever monster-hiding depths there might be down there.

From the way light rendered the material translucent, there wasn't anything under it.

She had a gun in her hand.

It was pointed at him.

"Arlo, you stupid son of a bitch," she acknowledged him with a rueful shake of the head. "It didn't have to end like this."

Yeah, yeah, it did, little girl.

Vo remained silent and still. His right side was towards her, but any sudden movements would get him shot. She had picked up archery quickly for a newbie. He suspected her small arms skills were probably much better.

Fish in a barrel time, at his end of the room.

"Did you find what you were looking for, Mister Arlo?" a man's voice inquired.

Vo could just make out Demir past Phoebe's shoulder. He was wearing a fluffy gray robe remarkably like the one at Phoebe's apartment.

Casually, Vo stood slowly upright, keeping his body faced towards the desk, but shifting his weight backwards as he tried to look defeated and harmless.

Harmless enough. Republic of Aquitaine *Marine here, pal.*

"No, Demir," Vo replied. "I did not. I found my file. I was looking for hers."

"Mine?" Phoebe was perplexed. "Oh my God, you really are a clueless one, aren't you?"

Vo watched her take an unconscious half-step forward, out of the hallway and into the doorframe space. He would have never done that, but those instincts had been knocked out of him by experts, years ago.

Always retain freedom of movement in all three dimensions.

"You don't get it, do you, you dumb lug?" she asked.

Vo still couldn't get to her without getting shot, he knew that, but Demir couldn't see anything over her shoulder without getting up on his tiptoes.

Vo shook his head mutely.

"I guess not," he replied quietly.

"He wasn't blackmailing me, you oaf," she sneered. "I'm his partner."

"Sorry I misunderstood, then, Phoebe," he observed quietly, letting things turn sour in his head, and his voice. "I thought you wanted a gentleman in your life."

Vo figured that the chances of her shooting him for that comment were pretty low. After all, she hadn't thrown the lemonade in his face earlier today, so she had self-control when she was angry.

Still. Stick the knife in, twist it, break it off.

The enemy is the enemy.

Her eyes did narrow angrily at his words, before softening some.

"And you were, Vo," she said in a quieter, warmer tone before the angry returned. "But this is about power, something you wouldn't understand, you Republican poodle. About building an entire network of people willing to pass me secrets. The kinds of money and favors that the *Fribourg Empire* pays us for access to all of it."

Vo nodded. Somewhere in the back of his mind, he had suspected.

Pretty girls and dragons.

At least it cleared up where everybody stood.

Now he had to get out of here alive.

"So now what?" he asked her simply.

It was the first time those words had come out of his mouth with this woman. The other opportunities had potentially opened too many risks. Dangerous ice.

It couldn't get any thinner right now.

"Now?" she snarled quietly. "You're going to come out of there quietly. We'll take you down to the basement and tie you up while we figure out what to do with you."

In his head, Vo silently translated. *We'll kill you and then find a vehicle and friends big enough to drag your sorry ass out into banjo country for the coyotes to eat.*

She had that mad dog look in her eyes.

Vo had a thing about dogs.

He let go of a defeated sigh and nodded before he slowly pivoted to his right, watching her eyes.

Phoebe was sharp. She was keyed up. She was almost good enough.

She took a step backwards and bumped the doorframe as she moved.

Her eyes blinked off his unconsciously as she stumbled, ever so slightly.

Vo brought his left hand up as he moved forward, towards the desk.

Her shot went wide. She had been expecting him to lunge away from the desk to get space to maneuver. It was a slug-thrower of some sort. Loud and with a tongue of flame as long as his hand.

The window behind him exploded.

Vo shot her dead center with the taze-pistol.

It was supposed to be able to take down a man his size. She was half his mass. Sudden muscle contraction put two more bullets into the wall and the ceiling as she collapsed backwards.

Vo sprang across the space as she fell. He had no idea if Demir was armed and didn't want to give the man any chance.

Again, owl and vole.

Vo was on top of him before the pudgy professor realized what was happening. Phoebe's pistol hadn't even landed on the carpet yet. Demir was unarmed.

Vo lashed out and punched the little professor as hard as he could, closed fist to the forehead. Exactly what you weren't supposed to do in melee combat, but he wanted the man down, not dead.

There were at least five other ways to hit the little professor from this position if he wanted the little man dead.

The vole went down twitching. Not out of it, like her, but stunned. Probably severely concussed. No longer a serious threat, if he ever had been.

Not like Phoebe.

Vo leaned over and hit Demir again, fist to the hard forehead bones. Just in case. And just because.

The floor echoed like a drum from Demir's skull bouncing off of it.

Vo pivoted and grabbed the girl's pistol from the floor where it had fallen. Slug-thrower. Internal box clip. Ambidextrous safety.

He wasn't familiar with the exact model, but it felt like it still had a half dozen more bullets inside. Vo set the safety and tucked it into his side pocket.

He grabbed the unconscious, twitching girl and dragged her into the open. With nothing better at hand, he pulled the linen shift over her head and used it to tie her wrists in front of her, where he could see them as he talked to her.

There really was nothing under that thin piece of cloth.

Then he moved on and used the belt from Demir's robe to tie him as well. The professor had nothing on underneath, either.

The robe reeked of Phoebe's perfume.

That was what he had smelled earlier.

Her. Here. The last place he had expected her.

Blind. Just like all the rest of the dumb marines.

The dangers of pretty girls.

Sirens calling sailors onto the rocks to crash and drown.

For a moment, he nearly let his anger get the better of him. He considered just shooting them both, right here, right now. Haul them into the woods and feed them to a pack of hungry coyotes.

Vo pulled out Phoebe's pistol and considered the cold, lethal weight in his hand.

Life and death. Eyes for eyes. Shooting them would be nicer than letting the experts at Fleet or Republic Intelligence get hold of these two.

At least, a cleaner way to die.

Navin's voice snapped him cold.

By the book, punk. It exists for a reason. Use it. Understand it. Master it. Then we'll talk.

He moved a little off and watched instead.

Phoebe stirred.

Her eyes opened, found him, focused.

The mad dog was back.

Vo considered punching her as hard as he could. There was a lot of anger sitting handy, just waiting for an excuse.

Any excuse.

By the book, punk. It exists for a reason. Use it. Understand it. Master it. Then we'll talk.

"So now what?" she sneered at him from some grand, intellectually-superior distance.

Vo felt that same distance engulf him as well.

"Now?" he answered quietly. "Now you discover what it means to lose, little girl."

"Is that supposed to frighten me, Arlo?" she hissed. "Because you've been a failure so far. But I guess you're always a failure around girls, aren't you?"

Vo shrugged.

You didn't argue with mad dogs.

From his back pocket, he pulled out his personal comm and dialed one of those emergency numbers they made you memorize without ever writing down.

A woman answered on the second beep.

"Whiskey," she said.

Nothing more. No emotional loading behind the word. Just two syllables.

Vo answered with a very specific sequence of apparently random gibberish. He took a breath and repeated Demir's address.

"Very good, Mr. Arlo," she replied. "ETA six minutes."

And the line went dead.

He stared at Phoebe. Her body was still the most utterly magnificent thing he had ever seen. Those brilliant green eyes were closer to normal. Maybe the mad dog was on a leash.

There was some confusion in there now.

Uncertainty.

The beginnings of fear.

Silence stretched.

"What's happening?" she whispered, after a spell.

He saw her glance over at the squishy professor, but the man was out and unlikely to recover his senses for a very long time. A good concussion did that to the brain. What was coming for him next would be the icing and the cherry, at least as far as Vo was concerned.

It was just the two of them.

"Some people are coming," Vo replied calmly, quietly.

Talking to the mad dog in those eyes.

"They're going to take you away, Phoebe," he continued. "Eventually, you are going to tell them everything they want to know. How much pain that requires will be entirely up to you."

His jaw hurt from not grinding it.

"Kill me," she pleaded at him quietly. "Please, Vo. Do you have any idea what this will do to my parents?"

The voice was different. She sounded like the tired, scared girl who had crawled up into his lap and fallen asleep, once upon a lifetime ago.

"No. No, I don't, Miss Akkersdijk," he said, feeling that emotional gulf in his head, that great space between them, turn into a moat filled with red lava.

Silence filled the hallway.

"You could have taken me, you know," she whispered. The voice was still soft and innocent. "Had me."

Fragile.

Frightened.

He kept his counsel as the silence stretched.

"We could have gone away," she continued, picking up as if the conversation hadn't lagged at all. "Left *Quinta* and never looked back. Vo, please?"

He just shrugged.

"If I hadn't been your mission, little girl," he snarled quietly back, "You would have never even noticed me. Pretty girls don't ever see monsters like Arlo, except when they need something."

He bit back the rest of the tirade in his head.

She wasn't listening.

There was nobody home.

Her eyes had gone unfocused. They had that glassiness that happened when true shock sets in.

Maybe she never had been beaten, at anything.

His comm chirped.

"Arlo," he answered.

"Contact," a man's voice replied.

"Second story hallway," he stated flatly. "Two prisoners. Building has not been secured."

"Acknowledged."

The line went dead again.

Vo counted five in his head.

Downstairs, the back door exploded inward. A Rapid Response Team made remarkably little racket as they poured through the flaming wreckage and began to go room to room.

Vo set the pistol down and lifted his hands up so he didn't get accidentally shot. Demir was still out and the girl had retreated so far inside herself it might take drugs to blast her mind loose and bring her back to reality.

But she wasn't his problem anymore. Republic Intelligence would take her and the vole away now.

Then they could find out how many other fools had been compromised, had been turned by her pretty face and twisted into being spies for the *Fribourg Empire*.

Vo's jaw hurt from clenching.

A siren on the rocks, calling sailors like him to their doom.

At least he finally knew why the pretty girl had noticed him.

ABOUT THE AUTHOR

Blaze Ward writes science fiction in the *Alexandria Station* universe as well as *The Collective*. He also write fantasy stories with several characters and series, from an alternate Rome to epic high fantasy in the desert. You can find out more at his website www.blazeward.com, as well as Facebook, Goodreads, and other places.

Blaze's works are available as ebooks, paper, and audio, and can be found at a variety of online vendors (Kobo, Amazon, and others). His newsletter comes out quarterly, and you can also follow his blog on his website. He really enjoys interacting with fans, and looks forward to any and all questions—even ones about his books!

Never miss a release!
If you'd like to be notified of new releases, sign up for my newsletter.

I only send out newsletters once a quarter, will never spam you, or use your email for nefarious purposes. You can also unsubscribe at any time.
http://www.blazeward.com/newsletter/

ABOUT KNOTTED ROAD PRESS

Knotted Road Press fiction specializes in dynamic writing set in mysterious, exotic locations.

Knotted Road Press non-fiction publishes autobiographies, business books, cookbooks, and how-to books with unique voices.

Knotted Road Press creates DRM-free ebooks as well as high-quality print books for readers around the world.

With authors in a variety of genres including literary, poetry, mystery, fantasy, and science fiction, Knotted Road Press has something for everyone.

Knotted Road Press
www.KnottedRoadPress.com

Be sure to read the first three volumes of The Jessica Keller Chronicles!

Auberon
Queen of the Pirates
Last of the Immortals

www.ingramcontent.com/pod-product-compliance
Lightning Source LLC
Chambersburg PA
CBHW071840190726
48292CB00005B/1849